TALES OF
NEW MEXICO

D1359896

Tales of New Mexico

by

Joseph D'Lacey

Black Shuck Books
www.BlackShuckBooks.co.uk

First published in the UK by Black Shuck Books, 2017

978-1-913038-07-6

7
The Gathering of Sheaves

65
The Vespertine

The
Gathering
of Sheaves

"In the desert, there is earth and sky and silence. The spirits find peace here but the living encounter only torment."

Chigger Nine Wren
Anasazi Medicine Man (1820 – 1853)

The sunlight was still and total, like the reflection off some vast steel blade. Even under the brim of his hat, it was hard to see without squinting. Something flickered in his periphery.

A bird?

Nicholson turned toward the movement and heard a rising whistle. The sound ceased as something punched him in the guts, causing him to cough. Even in the searing light, he could see the shaft of the arrow, carved with swirling glyphs, protruding from his abdomen.

He looked in the direction the flights of the arrow pointed. Nothing moved in the desert. He took the knife from its sheath in his belt and slit open his shirt. Blood seeped modestly from the wound, its lips tight to the body of the arrow. He bent to inspect it and the wound bubbled. He turned his nose away. When he looked back, a watery broth of faeces had turned his blood brown.

He folded to his knees and fell to his side, his hat rolling free.

From the brush in the distance rose a figure. It stood still. In time its shadow lengthened.

~

April 5th 1853
Langtry
Texas

After lodging in a hostelry by the name of Hogan's, the most flea-ridden establishment I have yet encountered, I am exhausted and no longer certain how far west I can travel whilst yet retaining my manners and my sanity.

I was obliged to share a dormitory with three fragrant cattlemen – shitkickers, as they proudly refer to themselves – who snored and broke wind with such ferocity the stench would have kept me awake if the noise hadn't. I fear my own alimentary canal will soon be similarly compromised. This morning, I was once again served pork and beans to break my fast. Before I could protest, two raw eggs were stirred into the brown mess. Without nourishment, I will faint in the constant heat but already I feel the growls of objection from within. I would give my silver timepiece for an apple, I swear it. I itch from scalp to soles with uncountable insect bites and my spine is sore from the warped pallet which served as my bed.

These are observations, not complaints, I hasten to add. A gentleman, particularly an Englishman treading unfamiliar soil, must keep his discomforts to himself. I am an ambassador merely by my presence in this country and I note my circumstances for posterity, not because I am frail or trepid.

It is a short walk from Hogan's to Langtry's only tavern – referred to as a saloon in these environs – where I hope to ask local men about the cactus. In particular the lawman who owns the establishment; a Judge Roy Bean, who oversees arrests and sentencing in this area. I have been told he is more than familiar with this wilderness and that he may be well-informed regarding local flora.

~

White light. White heat. An ache the size of a boulder swelling in his abdomen.

Nicholson rolls onto his back and groans as the ache sharpens; a giant fishhook tugging on his guts. Glare-blind, he reaches out for his hat, his fingers finding rocks, thorns and the hairlike spines of succulents. Something hard scuttles away when his fingers touch it and he snatches his hand back. No hat.

A shadow falls across him.

Squinting up, all he can see is the black shape of a man between him and the sun. The figure crouches and touches his wounded belly. Nicholson draws breath to scream but the man-shadow's knife blade steals his cry as it slides in deep beside the shaft of the arrow. The fishhook is removed.

He tries to scream again but the light of the world goes out.

~

April 5th 1853
Langtry
Texas

"All you'll find west of the Pecos is lawlessness and Indians. Pray you don't find 'em on the same day."

The first words out of Roy Bean's mouth when I attempted to explain what I was looking for. The man was short, potbellied and unwashed. Streams of yellow tainted his white beard and moustache and his clothes were bleached pale by sun and dust. He carried some great, unspoken weight in every wrinkle and looked as dead as the desert save for the oases of his eyes. If I'd met him on the fair streets of Glastonbury, I'd have taken him for a vagrant but in this realm he was judge, jury and executioner.

I say they were his first words. He looked at me for a long time before he spoke them, ruminating on some unseen mass, and produced a jet of black spittle, absorbed immediately it touched the parched earth. He gazed out from the uneven porch of his whisky-stocked courthouse into the expanse of nothingness beyond.

It was only then that he fixed me in those viper-quick eyes and made his pronouncement. I waited for more information but the man had nothing more to offer.

"My investigations are entirely... botanical in essence, Judge Bean. A serious pursuit which will further natural history and likely enrich the spirit of man. I am not a trouble-maker and I do not aim to fall foul of any blackguards – lawless, native or otherwise."

For a moment, the man looked surprised. But a hot breeze tugged at his wild, stained beard and he fell prey once more to the heavy scowl, forced upon him, it seemed, by the weight of the sky.

"Aim's got nothing to do with it."

He sat down on a three-legged stool beside an upturned barrel and lifted a jug of liquor to his lips with both hands. But to me he spoke not another word.

~

Nicholson wakes to agony.

Though the brightness of the day has faded

into twilight, his face is awash with sweat and his blood aflame. The pain in his belly is worse and it swells with every fevered beat of his heart. A smouldering mound of orange coals glows nearby. Beside the fire he sees the man, still only an outline in the half-light, the man whose crude surgery has wounded him more deeply than the arrow.

Hunched over, the silhouetted man whispers; a halting, guttural intonation without rhythm. Vowels and consonants that make no sense. He sways now, working on something in front of him. The words become a mumbled song, some kind of incantation or prayer.

Nicholson tries to speak.

"Water."

The rocking man doesn't answer.

"Please."

The man glances over and speaks; from the tone, some kind of command. He remains sitting, working on his primitive project.

Too weak to ask again, Nicholson can only watch, afloat on thirst and pain.

Hours later the silhouette approaches. He raises Nicholson's head and holds a bowl to his lips. Nicholson drains its contents before retching and coughing, eyes wide. The spasms send lightning bolts through his wound and he blacks out for a moment.

When he resurfaces, the pain has eased a little and the fire in his head has receded. The sun has set and the orange glow of the fire illuminates his benefactor. A young Indian with an old man's manner, lean but powerfully built. Nicholson sees loss and knowledge in eyes too ancient for such a youthful face.

"Thank you."

"For what?"

"The medicine."

The Indian laughs. In the quiet and creeping chill of evening, the sound is gone too quickly, taken by the desert.

"Save your gratitude, white man."

"Am I going to die?"

The man looks into the settling coals.

"We've all got it coming."

The words stretch out, echoing as though through a tunnel. The fire's light burns brighter and expands. The cold caress of the night is like black liquid, soothing and terrifying, a tide with the power to drown a whole world. Nicholson forces the sensation away.

"You're a healer to your people?"

"I do what I can."

Nicholson rests his head back in the dirt. The darkening sky swirls.

"Thank the Lord. Wounded and saved on the same day. How fortune dabbles."

"If you truly believe in your god, you'll know it's not fortune, white man. This is fate. The healing of this wound may be beyond me."

"It's only an expression," murmured Nicholson. "I'm not religious." He frowns at the sky. Beneath him, the rocky ground seems to shift. "What did you say?"

"The arrow should have entered your right arm."

Francis tries to lift his head but a torpor has ensnared him. The sky presses him into the earth. He is sinking; being buried.

"You're the one who shot me?"

The Indian leans over, blotting out the awakening stars.

"There's no one else out here. Just you and me."

"Why?"

"You're searching for the tracks of the little deer."

The Indian's words echo and elongate.

Francis frowns again.

"I don't understand."

The Indian laughs.

"Such will be the epitaph of your people. Only the Great Spirit knows why he made the white man so stupid." The Indian stands up, scanning the night. "Why did you come to the desert?"

"I seek a plant. A succulent. People say it has the power to alter the perceptions of men."

"You have sought, white man, and you have found. None of this is an accident, whether you understand it or not."

~

April 11th 1853
Marfa
Texas

There is no doubt now, that I underestimated the vicissitudes this undertaking would engender. The terrain is strewn with sharp, broken stones hidden by a low scrub of skeletal thorn bushes, prickly pear and other cacti; a Hades for any equine. I have lamed one horse already. A man on foot would shred his legs in minutes no matter how carefully he trod. The heat in the day is dizzying and the chill of the night eats into the marrow. If you were to stand a block of the finest English oak in this landscape, it would be bleached and split within the week.

The settlers in Texas come from many countries. I have encountered Bavarians, Scotsmen, Austrians and Russians. The majority are either drunk or working themselves to death in order to live. Often both. This is no land of plenty. Immigrants die of disease or penury each day, often interred in unmarked graves along the barely broken trails. There are many churches, one or more in every small community, but Christianity's grip on this land is weak and is no substitute for food, water, shelter and safety – all of which are scarce. It is no surprise to me that the principles of society are so easy to dismiss in this wilderness. If there is a God here, the land and the sky are His left and right hands. They give little in the way of succour. This is a place of desperation, of unquenchable thirst, and the people who have travelled so far to be here yearn for the bosom of their homelands. You may number me among them.

As for my business here, it is far from completed. I have engaged the service of a guide. He is a tiny man, his wrinkled skin dark as an old hazelnut. His eyes appear huge in his tiny face, stretched wide all the time, as if in wonder at the world. He speaks no English but often repeats a Spanish affirmation when I question him about plants unknown to me or comment on some quirk of the landscape. I therefore refer to him as Sisi. I have no idea if he is Mexican, Indian or from somewhere much farther south.

The hostelry in Marfa is better appointed than many I've made use of. I offered my guide a room on our arrival but he declined to cross the threshold, shaking his head and whining si, si until I lost patience with him. Let him sleep under his mule if that is what he wishes to do.

The bed-frame was iron, the mattress sprung, if a little soft. And though the whole structure creaked when I lay down, I knew I would rest like the dead.

I was wrong. At some unholy hour of the night, long after the poker players had left and the harlots snored as loudly as their clients, I woke to silent lightning. Each white flash left me blinded for a few moments, anticipating thunder that never came. I swung my legs from the bed and pushed open one of the shutters on the window. Miles out in the desert, cobalt blue pinpricks floated in the black sky, each one turning the world white with a single flash every few moments. The night was utterly still; I believed myself struck deaf at first. And yet, when I moved, I heard the creak of the floorboards. It was in some kind of mental haze then, caused, I assume, by exhaustion, that I simply tired of watching the display, lay down and slumbered until long after dawn.

As I attended to my horse and repacked the equipment and supplies, Sisi watched me from under the brim of his straw hat, glancing away each time I caught his eye. When we left Marfa, his pace betrayed an eagerness not apparent on the previous day.

~

The sky is black velvet, sewn with innumerable diamonds. Its weight compels Nicholson down into the rocks and dust of the desert. The land closes over him, the earth crushing him as the sequined night turns black. He tries to scream, but grit and stone fill his mouth, rill into his throat and nostrils.

From above, muffled and far away, comes the voice of his assassin.

"You must see, white man. And for that you must be reborn. Go into the belly of Grandmother Earth. Find your eyes."

As Nicholson sinks deeper, the earth squeezes him end to end until he is concertinaed, his knees forced to his chest. The compression on his wound is unbearable, pushing blood and partially formed excrement from the slit in his enflamed peritoneum. Dirt invades his ears, streams down his throat filling his lungs and stomach. The sharp edges of rocks cut into him. All his breath is gone.

~

April 14th 1853
Eddy
New Mexico Territory

Sisi's trail skills are astonishing and make up for his less endearing habits almost entirely. He has brought us into the New Mexico territory with far greater alacrity than I anticipated, often relinquishing the obvious route and taking us on detours that have saved us many hours of travel.

Each night and morning he prepares a fire for coffee and has caught several jackrabbits and other small mammals which he roasts for me over the coals. He does not share my meals, however, preferring to chew on some comestible he keeps in a leather pouch. When night falls and I am ensconced in my bedroll, he performs elaborate prayer rituals, whispering his strange language into a stone and holding it to his ear as though it answers him. Oftentimes he raises his hands to the night sky. It unnerves me a little, I do confess, to observe this performance just before sleep.

I console myself with the knowledge that I am closing on my objective. Although the *Peotl* is known in Texas, I am given to understand it is far more common to the deserts in which I now find myself. Common, that is, for a rare, incalculably valuable succulent.

Last night my sleep was once again disturbed, not by flatulent cowherds or distant lightning, but by a reverie. I would call it a dream but that it seemed so entirely real and yet I know such things cannot be. A reverie it must, therefore, remain: I heard the sound of footsteps, like the scamper of children. On opening my eyes, I saw many figures about me, flitting fast against the starry sky. I tried to call out to Sisi but could not. I have a small pistol – I was advised it was madness to travel here without such a weapon – but when I tried to reach for it, I was unable to move. My mind was alert and lucid but my body would not respond to any command. I have never known such helpless desperation. The small figures approached and I rose from the ground as though they had lifted me, yet I felt no hand upon my body. They bore me through the desert for a time, though I barely sensed the movement, so light-footed were they. There was brightness then, a light so bright it pierced my eyes, eyes I had not the strength to close. There the reverie appeared to end.

My next memory was of waking up with the dawn light, as stiff and sore as usual, with the chill of the night eating into my kidneys. I rose quickly and scanned our camp for signs of intrusion but there were none. Sisi looked up at me from the fire circle where he already had a good blaze going. I looked into his broad, staring eyes and shuddered. I have never given a moment's consideration to the plight of the paralysed but now the thought of such an affliction makes me nauseous with terror.

Sometime during the night I sustained a bite. Not from a mosquito or tick but something bigger. Sisi made scrabbling legs of his fingers when I showed him, signifying the movement of the desert tarantula, I assume. I now have a sore lump on my right upper arm, so swollen with venom it is hard to the touch. I showed Sisi my knife and made cutting motions next to the bite but he shook head his and waved his hands, crying "Si, si! Si, si!" which I took to mean that such bites are best left to heal on their own.

This valley, following the meanders of the Pecos, is a highway for cattle herders. We have been overtaken on two occasions by cowherds driving their bovine multitudes northwards, every animal ash-stained with the dust of the land. Though this activity makes the trail obvious and easy to follow, the sheer numbers force us to stop and make way. The windblown grit, great clouds of it sweeping after the herds, lodges in everything; hair, clothes and equipment. I have it in my mouth and ears. I have breathed it into my lungs.

Like Judge Roy Bean, like Sisi and all the other migrants I have encountered, I have the desert inside me now.

~

All movement ceases; breath, heart and thought compacted by the death grip of the earth.

Yet something abides, something witnesses.

After an incalculable interval, Nicholson realises it is he who watches in the dark, present but disembodied, sensing without participating, unable to do anything other than attend. For the first time in his life, he is unconcerned by any issue. He is at peace.

He hears faint thunder, feels it vibrate his awareness. The thunder becomes a slow pounding, distant but approaching until it is inside him; his heart beating stronger than before, to a new rhythm. The crushing begins again, but this time forcing him upwards. Nicholson fights it; the simple awareness was heavenly compared to this physicality, this rough intimacy. He rises head first, unable to resist the earth's contractions.

"No!"

His cry is swallowed by the rocks and dust.

His head breaks the surface and the sear of sunlight blinds him. Too weak to move, he lies face down on the hard ground, his face buried in the crook of his arm to keep out the light as the earth seals below him.

"Might be an idea to stand up, white man."

A hand takes hold of his upper arm and hauls him to his feet. He uses his free hand to cover his eyes.

"Hurts, doesn't it?"

Nicholson nods.

"Wait until you open them."

~

April 15th 1853
Pandemonium
New Mexico Territory

What a sight for travel-weary eyes. What rest for tired bones and insect-ravaged bodies.

Pandemonium!

Could there be a more ill-considered moniker for such a well-appointed town? It is like an Eden at the very end of the world. I believed it a mirage, at first; a sign I'd spent too long in the desert. Even Sisi, bringing his mule to an abrupt halt, appeared taken aback by the sight of the buildings rising from the horizon like images on a fluttering canvas. Truly, in the shimmer of rising heat, the place did not seem real.

And yet, some time later, we rode across the boundary, the town's name freshly painted across its timber arch, and onto Main Street. In other towns we'd passed through, curiosity about strangers and new arrivals was signified by a quick glance; two new morsels into the ravening maw of the American West were of no consequence. We posed no threat, carried no mail, held no promises. In Pandemonium, it was different. Eyes followed us. Faces appeared at windows. Figures stepped from doorways to watch. I sensed no hostility, not even suspicion. It seemed the inhabitants of Pandemonium assessed us with nothing more than resignation.

Yes, the town is crushed and besieged by the climate. There are glassless windows, warped porches and broken shingles on some of the roofs. But Pandemonium is alive, deep-rooted, and fights the elements for its place in the desert. Considering how difficult it must be to supply this place, I have nothing but admiration for its founders and citizens.

As we passed the jail, the sheriff stepped into view. He was a tall man, his dark moustache exaggerating the downturned corners of his mouth. The invasive oiliness of his gaze caused me to clench my teeth. His thumbs were hooked into his belt, the bony fingers of his right hand tapping the handle of a long, holstered pistol. In spite of passing through more towns than I can recall and being looked-over a thousand times, being scrutinised by the sheriff of Pandemonium marked the first instance I felt any real threat. Rather than leave my intentions to his imagination, I reined in my horse and raised my hat to the man.

"Good afternoon, Sheriff."

If the man nodded, I didn't catch the movement.

"My name is Francis Nicholson, of the county of Somerset in England and this is my gui—"

"I know who you are."

I'm sure my surprise was more than evident. I suppressed the urge to ask exactly how he knew.

"Then you'll know my business here is of an entirely–"

"Drink all you want. Gamble all you want.

Whore all you want. Step out of line just one time in Pandemonium and I'll send you home in one of Haight's boxes. It'll be a tight fit. He don't like to waste good wood."

I swallowed at the mere mention of enclosure, of immobility. A bead of sweat ran down my cheek. My face blazed at my weakness before this serpent of a man. However, I respect the law. It was, perhaps, the same law that preserved this town; prevented it from falling into chaos and ruin.

"I will endeavour to remember that, Sheriff, on each occasion I consider stealing a horse or shooting someone in cold blood. Tell me, if it isn't too much trouble, where might a dangerous gentleman such as I find lodgings in this fine town?"

The sheriff watched me for a long time, his unctuous gaze sliding all over me, his skeletal fingers still drumming at his gun. All the while, Sisi picked at the felt blanket that was his saddle, and hummed some unintelligible tune.

The sheriff signalled up Main Street with a glance.

"Café de Paris. Best hotel in Pandemonium."

~

While Nicholson's eyes adjust, unfamiliar sounds and scents assail him.

The dusty desert air has gone. Now he smells some kind of smoke, like burning paraffin. Wafts of sewage and the aroma of cooking mingle in the tainted air. His eyes register movement, people hurrying all around him. A rushing of air as loud, heavy objects hurtle past.

His vision clears and he gasps. He stands at the bottom of a valley with vertical sides. The valley is formed by buildings so tall he has to crane his neck in search of their roofs. Glass and metal gleam everywhere. Smooth-bodied horseless carriages flash by; too fast for him to inspect. And the noise, too loud and confusing to make sense of, is deafening.

He looks for a place to shelter but his assassin takes his shoulder in an eagle's grip.

"What's the matter, white man?"

"Is this hell?"

"Yes. Hell on Earth. Seven generations away."

Nicholson cowers, shaking.

"I'd be most grateful if you could take us away from this place."

"I wouldn't do that even if I could. *Peotl* is its own journey and its own map. This is where the tracks of the little deer have brought you. I can only be your guide."

Nicholson reaches for the Indian's hand, holds it with trembling fingers.

"Why is this happening to me?"

"Because you dreamed of it. Because you pursued it. Because seeing is the right of every man. Even the white man."

The ground begins to buzz, the vibrations tickling Nicholson's feet through his boots. The buzz becomes a tremor. The earth shakes and masonry impacts the street all around them. The milling people scream and try to run. The carriages go faster, many of them colliding. A fireball bursts from a ground floor window. Nicholson sees a woman hit by a chunk of stone almost twice her size. She simply vanishes. The quakes worsen and the earth bucks, sending Nicholson and the Indian into the air.

They float up, through the falling debris, rising past windows and roofs until they are high enough to see that the manmade valley is just one of many that crisscross each other, forming the heart of a city that stretches miles in every direction. Nicholson, who has never risen higher the third floor of a building, clings to the Indian like a baby to its mother.

The Indian smiles for the first time.

"*Peotl* will not allow you to fall. It wants you to see."

Nicholson feels the wind on his face. It strengthens to a gale. Only when he glances down again does he realise that he and the Indian are speeding through the air, leaving the city behind.

As they travel, his eyes are assailed by visions: he sees rivers, brown with sewage and the run-off from factories the size of towns. He sees the oceans, smothered silver-grey by a layer of dead fish that stretches to the horizon. He sees fire sweeping from forests into towns. He sees people of every nation dying of hunger and thirst. He sees London, ruined and abandoned.

The wind dies and they are standing once more on solid ground. Nicholson's eyes refocus on their surroundings. All is silent. Everything is broken. Through the destruction, he recognises the shapes of the street where they stood moments before.

"We have returned."

"No. We haven't moved – except through an age. This is eight generations hence."

"Where are the people?"

The Indian looks between the shattered buildings, gesturing into the distance.

"Gone to the harvest."

Nicholson smiles with relief, seeing the logic. People have moved from cities back to the land. He is able to admit to himself for the first time that he never really liked London, preferring the gentle valleys and rolling hills of his beloved Somerset. Throughout the journey to the desert he has tried hard not to think of home. Now the thought of it pierces him with longing. Though he is not God-fearing, the harvest in Glastonbury is his favourite season, a time of feasting, wassailing, music and dance.

The Indian moves off through the rubble. Afraid to be alone, Nicholson follows.

~

April 16th 1853
Pandemonium
New Mexico Territory

"Café de Paris is the only hotel in Pandemonium," said its proprietor, a Mr. Cathal Whelan, when I mentioned the esteem in which the sheriff held his establishment.

As obtuse and stubborn as many of the people I've met on this expedition have been, the sheriff of Pandemonium is the first to whom I've wanted to do violence. I can abide a drunk, a lecher – even a thief, if he be starving – but a man who abuses etiquette undermines the very fabric of society. Perhaps it is simple despotism that gives the sheriff such authority over this jewel in the wilderness.

"You can have your pick of the rooms, Mr. Nicholson. No other persons are residing with me at this time."

Mr. Whelan – "folks call me Cat" – retained some Galway inflections in his accent. He was a bent twig of a man and there was something simian about the way he scuttled along the hotel's creaking corridors, beckoning me to follow. After inspecting several rooms and finding them all equally dusty and bewebbed, I took a room that overlooked Main Street.

"We have a bathhouse, Mr. Nicholson. Doesn't see much use these days – other than for Mr. Calhoun's weekly visit – but I'd be happy to heat some water for you. You uh... look like the desert's been chewing on you."

I peered at the man. He swayed and shuffled

from foot to foot unceasingly. Unfeasible tufts of greying hair sprouted from his nose and ears, and his eyes seemed to show animal rather than human intelligence.

"I can think of nothing I'd enjoy more, Mr. Whelan."

The crooked man's head twitched on his shoulders.

"It's Cat."

I was relieved when he left the room, the little Irish gibbon.

From the window, Main Street appeared still. Whoever had watched us enter the town had now retreated. It was understandable: who would stay outdoors in this heat? Sisi was watering his mule and my horse at a trough near the hotel's entrance – forcing water up from far below, judging by the effort it took – with a hand pump. While they drank, he stood back and extracted some morsel from his leather pouch, glancing up and down the street before placing it in his mouth. When our mounts ceased to drink, he led them to the side of the hotel where I lost sight of him.

I have had some discomforts along the way and endured my share of delays and minor mishaps. To arrive in Pandemonium, to know the thing I seek may be within walking distance of the faded glory of this hotel, it feels a little like destiny to me. I know how fanciful it will seem to say it, but it strikes me that this is a journey I was fated to make. And with that sense comes a certainty, entirely devoid of logic, that I will find the object of my search, study it and bring it back to England – for king, for country and for the good of mankind.

But first, a most welcome and overdue ablution.

~

Nicholson sees blue-white explosions within the bellies of corpulent clouds. He waits but there is no thunder. The lightning bursts at regular intervals, far in the distance, flashing the broken cityscape into grey white relief as they pick their way through the destruction.

"I've seen this. In the desert."

"This is different, white man. This is worse."

Nicholson stops walking. The Indian turns. Nicholson proffers his hand.

"I know this is a vision and that I'll wake up and feel as foolish as a schoolboy but I'd like to know your name. And I'd rather you stopped calling me white man. I'm Francis Nicholson."

The Indian walked back towards him and took his hand.

"My people call me Nine Wren. White men call me Chigger."

"Chigger?"

"It is their name for an insect which burrows under the skin to breed. They consider me an irritation."

"I must confess to a similar sentiment."

"Then you must call me Chigger... Francis Nicholson. Quick now, or we will miss the harvest."

Chigger turns away and quickens his pace. Nicholson follows. Soon they are running, fast and without any strain, leaping heaps of rubble, ducking under fallen girders. They swiftly close the distance between themselves and the bright, silent clouds. Chigger leads them into a high, windowless building and Nicholson counts fifteen flights of stairs as they sprint up. The Indian vanishes through a doorway and Nicholson follows. They emerge onto the flat roof and Chigger drops low, creeping to the edge. Very slowly, he peers over. Nicholson peeps over too. A soundless flash illuminates the night. By its afterglow, Nicholson sees a procession of people walking from the city into a featureless expanse – a plain without grass, utterly flat. Utterly unnatural. The lightning glow fades before he can discern much more.

"I can't make it out. What are they doing?"

"Dawn will show it to you. Rest a while."

Chigger puts his back to the low wall around the rooftop and relaxes. Nicholson does the same. But he can't settle. He turns to Chigger.

"We build a new world and we destroy it. That's why you're showing me this, isn't it?"

Chigger laughs without a trace of humour.

"That we could fix, Francis Nicholson. Perhaps. We could fix it by killing all the white men in the world and laying their stupid ideas to rest forever. This is something far worse."

"I don't understand."

Chigger smirks.

"You will."

Nicholson considers for a while, trying to ignore the Indian's disdain.

"You speak English very well... for a—"

"Savage?"

"That wasn't what I was going to say."

"I can assure you, Francis Nicholson, that you hold me in far greater contempt than I hold you. Whether you admit it to yourself or not." Chigger reaches into the leather satchel and brings out a corncob pipe and a pouch of tobacco. He loads the pipe and lights it with a match, drawing smoke with almost sexual satisfaction. "I've learned everything I can about the white man. His language. His desires. The broken way he thinks." Chigger offers the pipe to Nicholson, who shakes his head. "I've even taken up some of his stupid habits to help me understand him better. We may both bleed when cut but I've come to the conclusion that we are different on the inside, the red man and the white. The red man's roots are in the earth but yours are in the sky. Somehow this world makes you blind whilst it allows us to see. And so, Francis Nicholson, that is why you had to find new eyes. *Peotl* is the eyes of the earth and the earth wants you to see. Now. Before it's too late."

~

April 17th 1853
Pandemonium
New Mexico Territory

"An Englishman? What the juice is an Englishman doing in my bathhouse, Cat? I'm all the English this town will ever need."

"Sorry, Mr. Calhoun. He's a paying guest of the hotel. And he smelled kinda ripe on arrival."

Until that moment, my bathe had been sublime. Not quite a proper English bath – which I'm sure Mr. Calhoun is an expert on – but warm and wet and renewing, nonetheless. I sighed and hoisted myself from the filthy marinade I'd created, towelled vigorously, taking extra care around the spider bite, and slipped back to my room before Mr. Calhoun could confront the English imposter in his already English-enough town.

Most of the heat had gone out of the day and I was still curious about Pandemonium. When I was sure Mr. Calhoun had vacated the premises, I slipped back down the stairs and rung the bell for Mr. Whelan at reception. He appeared from below the counter, giving me a start.

"Yessir?"

"I'd like a meal," I said. "Meat. Potatoes. Vegetables if you have them. No pulses or legumes."

"Legumes?"

"Beans. I don't want beans."

"No beans."

"I'm going to take a brief constitutional. Is an hour long enough?"

"Long enough for what?"

"To prepare my repast."

Cat glanced around, as though at some flying insect. He looked back at me.

"Can I help you, sir?"

I felt my face flush but breathed before speaking.

"Does an hour give you long enough to prepare the food, Mr. Whelan?"

"Cat." He smiled a yellow-toothed smile. "Sure it does. Anything else I can do for you?"

"Make it two meals, please."

I found my guide sitting under his mule in the hotel stable, ruminating. It must have been a tough mouthful.

"I have requested that the hotelier cooks you a proper meal. Will you join me for dinner?"

He tried to speak but his mouth was stoppered. Finally he swallowed, rolling his eyes up as he did so, and then looking back at me, something akin to guilty humour in his expression. He didn't speak.

"Are you hungry?" I made signs with my hands. "This man will make us good food. Do you want to eat?"

"*Si, si! Si, si!*"

I sighed.

"Come inside in one hour." I showed him my pocket watch, held up my index finger. "One hour. Understand?"

"*Si, si!*"

It was a relief to leave him in the cramped stable and stand once more in Pandemonium's Main Street. It was broad and surprisingly free of debris. Most towns had middens of waste along each side, where children found junk and brought it to life with their imaginations, where rats foraged. But this street was clear. From time to time a lazy dust devil spun the sandy dirt into a funnel and carried it away.

The town seemed deserted now as I sauntered in the evening haze, and yet I was unable to shake that sense of being secretly observed. Not one of Pandemonium's establishments showed any sign of occupation; even the saloon was silent. I thought perhaps the custom here might be to come out after sunset when the air was cooler but it was hard to ignore the idea that I was somehow the fool here, abroad at some dangerous hour of the day. These thoughts spoiled my walk and sent me back to the Café de Paris where I sit and write this in the once glorious but now shabby lounge.

Later

Cat Whelan called me a good half hour after the agreed time. Sisi had not appeared so I went back to the stables to fetch him. He was still under his mule, still chewing. I explained that our food was ready. He grinned. I beckoned him inside the hotel. He nodded. I lost my temper.

"It'll be bloody cold if you don't come now, man!"

"*Si, si!*" He said.

But he didn't budge.

On returning to the large, deserted dining room, I found two pewter bowls of pork and beans. From the kitchen, I was certain I heard a stifled giggle.

~

Dawn arrives, its creeping grip more like the spread of an infection than the arrival of the sun. By its grey light, Nicholson sees the harvest procession more clearly. Exhausted people stumble from the city in their thousands, their faces lowered in shame or defeat. They are naked and troop in unison, as though to some unheard command.

When the sky brightens a little more, Nicholson sees another column far out in the flattened wasteland, this one populated entirely by cattle. Its head meets the head of the human procession, so distant as to be no more than a thread. Muted flashes continue from above.

"Where are they going, Chigger?"

"Into the belly of the silent thunderbird, into the belly of its masters."

"But why?"

Chigger reaches into his satchel, this time removing a small, leather-bound King James Bible. He flips to the last few pages.

"'And another angel came out of the temple, crying with a loud voice to him that sat on the cloud, Thrust in thy sickle, and reap: for the time is come for thee to reap; for the harvest of the earth is ripe.' Revelation. Chapter 14. Fifteenth verse."

Nicholson shrugs.

"If that's an explanation, I'm afraid I'm none the wiser for it."

"It is a prophecy. From the white man's god."

"I'm a man of science, Chigger, not a man of God."

"The same prophecy exists in Anasazi folklore, almost word for word. And in that of many other Indian nations."

Nicholson watches the mindless parade of humanity trudging away. The tail end of the column appears, leaving him and Chigger alone, and the broken metropolis descends into an even deeper silence. He glimpses a gargantuan shadow inside the distant thunderheads. Gooseflesh breaks out all over his body. A wash of nausea sweeps through him.

"Who is 'him that sat on the cloud'? Does it refer to God?

Chigger points into the voiceless lightning.

"It is that, Francis Nicholson. The silent thunderbird and the Grey Man who flies inside it."

A vast shape slips free of the clouds, its size freezing Nicholson with a kind of vertigo. The object is miles away and yet it is crushingly huge. It floats above the wasteland like a city.

"Why have they come here?"

"They have been among us for centuries

already.   Orchestrating,   managing, encouraging. They have made a farm of this world and everything that lives here has become their stock."

As he says the words, the heads of the columns lift like silk on a breeze, drawn up towards the craft above. It hauls on the threads, reeling them in. Nicholson realises he is holding his breath; the speed at which so many thousands of living things disappear upwards is beyond his grasp.

"This is a dream," he says. "From the cactus. I will wake up and the dream will be gone."

"It is real, Francis Nicholson. As real as your wound."

Nicholson glances down at the mention of it and the pain returns. He is leaking again. Blood, watery pus, a gruel of sewage. A wind springs up, tugging at them on their rooftop vantage. Chigger looks up at the touch of it.

"*Peotl* calls us home."

The building vanishes from under them, the entire city evaporates, and they fall twenty storeys. Nicholson screws his eyes closed. When he hits the ground, his eyes snap open. He is lying near Chigger's fire, its glow almost gone now. Chigger sits cross-legged beside him, eyes closed. The pain in his gut is rising like a drum-roll. As he calls out for Chigger to wake up, he hears something move a few yards away in the darkness; the clatter of a rock, loud and wrong in the otherwise hushed desert. By the scant glow from the fire, Nicholson sees Chigger's eyes open to a slit. Silent as smoke, the Indian puts his hand to his waist. The same hand blurs, up and outward. Some distance away, Nicholson hears a gristly snick of impact. Chigger leaps to his feet and disappears into the dark. Moments later, he returns dragging something heavy through the dirt.

"Jesus wept," says Nicholson. "You've murdered my assistant."

"You are not the master he serves. Coyote has tricked you."

A dark fluid seeps from the wound in Sisi's chest. Chigger removes his knife and uses it to cut into the wizened man's cheek. Nicholson manages to raise himself up on one elbow.

"Stop that now. What the devil do you think you're doing?"

Chigger continues to cut, opening a flap beside Sisi's nose and tearing the skin open.

Nicholson's further protestations are not aimed at Chigger Nine Wren but to the God in whom he has always professed not to believe. Beneath the face Nicholson has come to know, the face of a man he'd considered an ally if not an actual friend, there is a second face, smooth and slate grey, the cosmos reflecting in its dead almond-shaped eyes.

Nicholson collapses back. He begins to shiver as the pain in his abdomen increases and his face runs with sweat. No longer strong enough even to turn his head, he drifts in and out of consciousness to the sound of honed steel sawing through muscle and ligament.

~

April 18th 1853
Pandemonium
New Mexico Territory

I feel a certain reluctance this morning. I have no doubt that today will be the day I find what I seek.

Ever since I heard of *Peotl*'s existence, I have felt its pull. I am a man of science, a man of rational thought. Throughout my career, I have gathered, studied and measured flora in the most logical, impassive manner. That distancing is born of a love for the natural world and, most especially, its seemingly endless variety of plant life, the uses of which I believe we are only just beginning to understand. And yet, in this one instance, in this search for the *Peotl* cactus, I have acted on nothing but whim and instinct.

I *have a sense* about it. That is all.

I have a sense that this humble but rare cactus, with its alleged ability to open the eyes of men to a world even richer than that which we perceive, will be boon for humanity, a teaching tool that will help us to break free of ignorance and prejudice and the simple misapprehensions so many act upon each day. For the first time in my life, I have absolutely no basis for this assertion and yet it has become my prime motivation. Perhaps they will think me mad in London upon my return; perhaps even in my home of Glastonbury. But if *Peotl* has the properties I hope for, such appraisals won't persist for long. I do not wish to be celebrated by my peers, or even envied by them. However, if I am successful, then mayhap the common man of all nations, within and without the empire, will be exalted in wisdom and liberty: the liberty of truth.

Ah. My stomach gurgles. I do believe my body has become accustomed to this diet, even if my mind has not. I go to breakfast now, with a simple hunger and little in the way of expectations.

~

Nicholson awakes and the desert is silent. There is light but the sun has yet to clear the horizon. High above, buzzards glide in patient spirals.

All this way.

Nicholson turns his head. There is no sign of Chigger Nine Wren, no sign of a fire. There is the hard earth below him and the abyssal vault above. Nothing more. America. The most majestic land, the broadest sky he has ever seen. Tears seep from his eyes, run back past his ears, drip into the dirt.

All this way for a mortal wound and a fever dream.

Thankfully, he can no longer feel the pain. The flesh of his belly and his punctured innards will be necrotic and nerveless by now. All he has to do is wait and hope he goes before the desert scavengers move in on him.

Suddenly he is outraged.

"I did my best," he screams at the vacuum of the sky. "I remain an Englishman and a gentleman – *to the end*."

"The Great Spirit doesn't care about your manners or where you were born."

The voice comes from the one place he can't look in this position, north of his head. He cranes around to see Chigger squatting on his haunches, braiding something with deft fingers.

"How can you sit there and mock my final moments? You are a bloody savage."

"And proud of it. Grandmother and Grandfather know what's in my heart and they love me, for they were the first wild spirits here and I follow their lead."

"For God's sake, leave me alone."

"I can't do that. We need to go."

Nicholson closes his eyes and shakes his head.

"I can't go anywhere like this."

"You can and you must, Francis Nicholson. You have much work to do."

"I'm *dying*, you imbecile!"

Chigger springs up and hauls Nicholson to

his feet. Nicholson looks down at the ragged tear in his shirt; the blood, mucus and faeces that have dried there. He pulls the stained cotton up to inspect the wound. There is nothing but the smooth unblemished skin of his stomach.

Chigger holds up a silver, egg-shaped stone.

"The Grey Man has powerful healing."

Standing, Nicholson sees the cairn of dark, dismembered flesh and flayed ashen skin that had been the thing inside Sisi. The pile is topped by an eyeless, elongated skull.

"Why did you do that to him?"

"Sometimes they have... things inside them. The things must be removed. It's not always easy to find them."

Nicholson put his fingers to his forehead, shakes his head.

Chigger Nine Wren moves to his right side.

"Francis Nicholson?"

"For the love of Christ, man. What?"

"I hope you will forgive me."

Nicholson frowns.

"Forgi—"

Chigger pierces his upper arm with the tip of his knife. Nicholson leaps back, clapping his left hand over the wound. Blood wells between his fingers. His face whitens with fury. He reaches for the small pistol under his waistcoat and draws it.

Chigger stands eye to eye with him.

"You had a dream not long ago."

Nicholson raises the pistol, his arm shaking.

"Fever. *Peotl*. Whatever it was, I've had enough of your insanity."

"No, Francis Nicholson. Before this. In the night." Chigger nods towards the glistening heap of charcoal and slate-coloured meat. "Your guide would have been there. A dream of... oppression. Of paralysis. Do you remember?"

The pistol wavers.

"I... how did you—"

"They suspected you. They sent your guide and he led you – to them. He did nothing to stop them when they took you."

"Took me... where?"

"Into the silent thunderbird. They put something inside you, Francis Nicholson. I came here to take it out."

"Is that why you tried to kill me?"

Chigger shrugs.

"I was aiming for your arm. You moved."

"I almost died."

"I saved your life."

Nicholson grinds his teeth.

"I should shoot you where you stand."

"You wouldn't be the first white man to try." Chigger moves towards Nicholson. "I have to take it out. Or they'll follow you for the rest of your life."

Nicholson peers under the hand holding the cut in his arm. The exact location of the spider bite. He looks back at Chigger and lets his pistol drop to his side.

"Do it quickly, will you? I'm not sure how much more of this I can stand."

He feels Chigger's fingers at the edge of the wound before penetrating. He draws breath to scream when Chigger holds up a blood-smeared silver cylinder not much bigger than a rice grain. Before Nicholson can get a close look, Chigger puts his free hand into his satchel and pulls out a struggling lizard. He pinches its mouth open and thrusts the bloody thing into its gullet before releasing it into the dirt. It skitters away in a frantic dash for cover. Chigger presses his egg stone to Nicholson's cut, sealing the flesh instantly.

"Come," he says. "We must hurry."

April 18th 1853
Pandemonium
New Mexico Territory
Later

Let us not discuss my breakfast, other than to say I expect it will be among the last here in Pandemonium if today's ride goes the way I hope it will. Once I have collected specimens, noted habitat, soil composition and atmospheric conditions, I will make the journey east and depart for England, carrying my prize. I aim to reproduce this very climate under glass in my laboratory in Somerset and cultivate *Peotl* for the purposes of experimentation.

I may venture out alone this morning, as I am able to find no sign of Sisi. His mule is gone from the stable. I asked Cat Whelan if he'd seen the prune of a man but the hotelier smelled so terribly of whisky, I doubt he could see me properly, let alone events in the environs. It strikes me as queer; I have not paid my guide, for our contract is not yet complete. Perhaps he is observing some pagan rite in the desert, away from civilised eyes. I expect he will return later demanding recompense and I shall pay the man happily for his work. However, I plan to make the return leg of my sojourn alone. I am confident of the route and any concern about 'trouble' has been laid to rest by experience. As for Judge Roy Bean, no prophet is he; merely a liquor-soused layabout who sees evil under every rock.

The sky is almost white already, such is the blaze of the desert sun. I shall be sure to water my horse well before venturing out and will take a full canteen for myself, even though I expect to return no later than mid-afternoon. If there is any justice in this world, I shall find my prize today.

~

Nicholson, despite the healing of both his wounds, is unable to keep up with the Indian as he sprints over the uneven ground of the desert. Chigger runs with the grace of an animal. Nicholson stumbles often.

Chigger looks back, exasperated.

"Ask the earth to guide your footsteps, Francis Nicholson."

"What?"

Chigger smiles.

"Run faster."

"Where is my horse?"

"Run faster and you'll see sooner!"

Chigger dashes away again, his toes finding reliable purchase every time his feet touch the ground. The gap widens. Twenty yards. Thirty. Nicholson scans the horizon for some landmark or destination. The desert is vast and featureless.

"You must hurry," Chigger calls without looking back. "They will come."

"There's nothing out here."

Before the words are out of Nicholson's mouth, Chigger disappears as though the earth has swallowed him. More *Peotl* mind tricks? Nicholson blanches at the thought but keeps running. He sees the precipice only after it's too late to stop himself. As he flails over the lip he sees a ravine below, a small river, lush green trees and patches of grass. He sees Chigger trotting down a small track. The ledge is only six feet above the banked sides of the canyon. Though he stumbles when he hits the loose ground, Nicholson soon rights himself. He chases Chigger with new energy. It takes them ten minutes to reach the flat bottom of the canyon and the cottonwood tree to which their horses are tethered. The air is cool and fragrant down here. If it weren't for the steep walls of stone framing the scene, Nicholson might almost imagine himself home.

Chigger wastes no time mounting his horse and spurring it forward. Nicholson wants nothing more than to drink the river water, to bathe in it, but he follows the Indian's lead. They canter along the watercourse for several miles, the size of this hidden world causing Nicholson to gape. The canyon narrows, the trees thin and disappear, the river vanishes into stone.

Chigger reins his horse to a halt. Nicholson looks around.

"Why have you brought us here? It's a dead end."

Chigger turns back to him.

"Swear to me you will never speak of this place, Francis Nicholson, or we can go no further."

Nicholson gestures at the rock walls.

"There's nowhere else to go."

"Swear it."

"All right. I swear."

Chigger watches him for a long time. All Nicholson can hear is the rush of the water.

"This canyon is sacred to the Anasazi. Though we are a desert people, we come here sometimes, usually alone. It is a place of spirit and healing, near to Grandmother's heart. The caves lead back to the white man's town. That is where you must go."

Chigger takes out Sisi's leather pouch and hands it over. Nicholson opens its drawstring neck and reaches in. He removes a brown cube and sniffs it. It reminds him of salted pork.

"What is this?"

Chigger shrugs. "It is the fruit of the harvest, Francis Nicholson. You would call it jerky. The flesh of many creatures, mingled, spiced and cured. The flesh of my people. The flesh of yours. It is the Grey Man who is your enemy, not the Red Man. Do not forget this."

Nicholson swallows back a nauseous convulsion of his stomach and throws the pouch and its contents as far away as he can. Chigger passes him a second, larger pouch, similar to his own satchel. Nicholson looks at him.

"*Peotl*. Many plants and many seeds. Some

dried and some fresh. Samples of the soil from where they grew. I have written a list of instructions for its cultivation and how you must speak to the *Peotl* at the various stages of its development."

"Speak?"

"Surely you have seen enough now, Francis Nicholson, to trust me. To trust in the earth. The world is as you dream it. You must do what you were born to do."

Nicholson stares at the satchel.

"How did you... know about me?"

Chigger smiles.

"I listen to my grandmother."

For a while Nicholson doesn't know how to respond. The Indian has an answer for everything, even though Nicholson understands very little of what he says. He listens to the river water as it disappears into the rock wall and to the whisper of the trees further back along the river's course. Is there a voice in those sounds? He is about to ask but Chigger speaks first.

"You must go now, Francis Nicholson. Into the caves."

"What caves? There's nothing here."

"I think I understand now why the Great

Spirit made the White Man so stupid. It is because he has no stomach for the truth, even when it is right in front of him. The Great Spirit must know that when the White Man one day grows a strong stomach, he will finally find joy in this world."

Nicholson allows a memory of home to replace his frustration with the Indian's irritating chatter.

"And you, Chigger Nine Wren? What will you do?"

The Indian looks up into the sky over the canyon. A shadow plunges the narrow paradise into twilight. When he looks back at Nicholson, his face is grim.

"My destiny comes on the wind."

Chigger spurs his horse and it rears before galloping away, back in the direction from which they came. Nicholson sees the Indian draw a tomahawk and hold it high as he disappears between the cottonwoods. The shadow moves after him and Nicholson hears Chigger's war cry echo off the canyon walls. He turns his horse towards the rock wall and urges it forward but the horse, seeing nowhere to go, balks. He spurs it and the horse bolts forward. A slice of darkness appears, broadening as they approach. They are at the mouth of a tall, narrow cave, hidden by a quirk in the formation of the rocks.

Nicholson shakes his head, smiles and walks his horse into the black.

~

June 3rd 1853
Norfolk
Virginia

The paddle steamer *Neptune* leaves for Southampton tomorrow. Far greater than the anticipation of stepping once more onto English soil, I have no doubt, will be the relief I feel to leave America behind me. I can bear its stain no longer nor the phantoms that have pursued me these last six weeks, of which I have already written enough.

Suffice it to say that I am here, in a small hotel near the dock, my personal valise packed and my trunk already aboard in my cabin. I have spared no expense for the return crossing. I need privacy and rest. I plan to further my experiences with *Peotl* during the passage, following Chigger Nine Wren's compassionate and wise instructions as closely as I'm able.

How many times must I confess in these pages that I misjudged the man? That I held him in low regard because of his blood? I say it again here, wishing only that I might have behaved more like the gentleman I have always believed myself to be – and how wrong I have been about that, in addition – instead of allowing prejudice and contempt to get the better of me. This trait is, perhaps, the worst an Englishman can display and it is rife among us, we who believe ourselves masters of an empire.

The empire will not last. For a greater empire than men can imagine is already upon us. On each of the six occasions I have communed with *Peotl* during my journey east from Pandemonium, I have seen with the same eyes it gave me on that first day. It has become my guide. I see the Grey Man, disguised among us, and I see the many ways in which he has implemented his empire, laying his plans above and below ours so that we march directly into his baited trap.

I cannot and will not allow it to continue without resistance.

Chigger's final wish was for me to take *Peotl*

to the White Man, to give my people new eyes. For blind we cannot fight the Grey Man; we do not even know he is here. My plan is to introduce *Peotl* as a pharmaceutical that improves physical sight. Once its true effects have circulated among the more bohemian in London society, rumour will spread quickly. Provided I am able to cultivate enough psychoactive agent, *Peotl* will become as common as tea and will take its place in our culture the way it has among the Anasazi. I will bring new eyes to the British Empire so that all our nations may fight the Grey Man and send him back from whence he came.

Chigger's command of the English language was astonishing. I only realise it now, when I sit to study his instructions regarding the correct handling of *Peotl*. He is at all times precise and clear. I only wish I could have spent more time with him, knowing what I know now. In his letters, he intimates that we will meet again, in another form. But even my further forays into deep perception have not shown me what that might mean. I can only say that, if ever we are once more united, I shall embrace him as an equal, as a brother.

Nay, I shall beg for his forgiveness.

THE MORNING HERALD
FRIDAY MORNING, JUNE 10, 1853
LOSS OF AN AMERICAN PACKET SHIP

We (Morning Herald) have received intelligence this evening of the total loss of the American ship Neptune, Captain Furber, which sailed from Norfolk, Virginia on Friday last for Southampton. The Neptune was a fine ship, of upwards of 1000 tonne burden, and nearly new. The particulars of the occurrence, so far as we have been able to learn, are as follows:–

The Neptune sailed with forty passengers and a crew of thirty-three, proceeding safely until yesterday. A schooner Mirabel, Captain Hardwick, came upon the ship as it sank, seemingly without cause. None of the lifeboats had been deployed and there was no sign of passengers or crew.

Captain Hardwick reports seeing lightning in the hour before he came across the stricken vessel; however, he asserts that winds were moderate at all times. Neither he nor his crew saw any other sign of a storm and he could postulate no reasonable explanation for the Neptune's sinking.

Some luggage and personal effects have been salvaged but the cargo and all souls were lost.

The Vespertine

Wrapped in furs and a heavy blanket, his eyes reflecting the red embers of the fire, the old man studied the dark, lean stranger sitting opposite him. Around them, the desert whispered with nocturnal life.

Silently, and hidden from sight, the old man's hands unsheathed a long, worn hunting knife. He cradled it in his lap. The fire settled, sending up sparks, and the stranger flinched. From a pouch at his waist, the old man took a pinch of dried mushrooms mixed with dung, earth and blessed spring water. He worked the paste along his blade. The tented layers that covered him did not move nor did the prayers he breathed make a sound.

When he was prepared, the old man raised his attention from the fire. His face was kind but his skin was leathery, crushed by decades of sun and injustice. He let his eyes rest upon the stranger who had travelled so far in search of him and when the old man spoke, his voice was cracked and reedy.

"How well can you speak English?"

The stranger tensed.

"Do you insult me?"

"I want you to tell me, clearly, what it is you seek."

"You know what I want. How many ways are there to say it, *vecchio*? I come to you for healing."

The old man gazed back into the fire.

"So often our illnesses are our greatest teachers. In restoring your health, I may rob you of wisdom."

The stranger leaned forward, his eyes unwavering, their whites intense.

"With the very greatest respect, *vecchio*, I can assure you this illness is no such mentor to me. It is my curse and it has cost me everything. My dignity, my freedom... my faith."

The old man nodded.

"I understand. But all this *must* be spoken of first. The truth, as close as you are able to express it, must be heard."

The stranger's jaw rippled. The old man gripped the handle of his knife.

"I did not come here to *talk*."

The night swallowed the stranger's anger.

"Yes," whispered the old man. "You did. And talk you will or there can be no healing here."

The old man let his hands escape his heavy wrappings. Again the stranger flinched but when he saw the old man's pipe and pouch, his gnarled shaking fingers, he relaxed again.

"I don't smoke."

"Tonight, you do."

As he fumbled to fill the pipe's bowl, spilling a little of the sacred blend onto the ground, the old man spoke, and his voice was the kindest sound in the desert.

"There is a war inside you, stranger," he whispered. "Light against darkness. Day against night. Not the moral war that men and women fight within themselves each day. Something worse. Something eternal." He lit the pipe and handed it to the stranger. "Tell me your story. Every part. And maybe then we'll see."

The stranger watched the old man. For a long time, he did not move or speak. The fire settled again and the movement drew his gaze. His attention fused with the scant flames, their deep living glow, and a smile twitched the corners of his mouth; the smile of a man intimate with conflagration, who respects it.

When the stranger looked up at the old man, the fire lived on in his eyes. He took the pipe. Its bowl was carved white quartz; a crouching cougar married to a shaft of red cedar. Bright feathers adorned it and serpentine glyphs grooved the wood. The stranger paused, regarding the pipe, and then drew hard, pulling deep. He closed his eyes, releasing the smoke with a sigh. Some of the tension melted from his shoulders and face.

"Alright," he said. "I will tell it. I will tell you everything."

The stranger passed the pipe back, the unfamiliar fumes already causing him to sway. He took a determined breath and sat straighter.

"When I remember the chamber, *vecchio*, it is the fire I see. Always the fire. The doctor had built an incinerator within the very rock, drilling a crude chimney up into his house. There it joined the main flu of the fireplace he used to heat his drawing room. When he burned the bodies, the smoke of their remains joined that of the logs smouldering in his hearth. And his wife, either trusting or ignorant, suspected nothing.

"But I am rushing ahead. Telling you the end before the tale has even begun. Like the kiss of fire on naked skin, there is only so much I can stand. Let me tell it in pictures, *vecchio*. Snapshots of something catching fire, burning brightly, dying, cold."

They have held me down here for a hundred and forty-eight nights.

I cannot see the cycles of the sun and moon but I sense their tides of attraction and repulsion in every artery. There may be a hundred feet of rock between my body and the surface, but I know when midday comes; it makes my very cells prickle with loathing. Whereas midnight flows in my veins like some hallowed alchemy of morphine and quicksilver.

They come at night, of course, when the rest of the town sleeps.

They come wearing smocks, like butchers ready to labour with the cleaver and the block. They come to me with their tools and their instruments, their hands shaking with avarice and excitement. And they take what they want without so much as looking me in the eye.

Each dawn, I sense the sun regain its power over this part of the globe but, even before its heat thaws the desert stones, the evidence of their abominations has faded. By nightfall there is no trace of injury. I am renascent.

This alone gives me hope. For each day that they do not bleed me dry grants me another twenty-four hours in which to plot my liberation.

I first became unwell following a visit to my sister in Virgen, Austria in 1921. May all the saints forgive me.

The journey, one I've made each Easter since the Austro-Hungarian surrender of 1918, is a difficult one under the best circumstances. Only when the pristine teeth of winter unclench do the mountain roads and trails become accessible. It is close to three hundred kilometres from my cottage in Pieve on the western shore of Lake Garda to Julietta's hillside orphanage in that gloomy Austrian valley. The wounds of war, upon the landscape and its people, remain raw.

The treacherous Tyrolean passes are no place for a car but a strong horse, sufficiently fed and watered, can make the journey in less than two weeks. Despite the bloodshed and screaming artillery thunder of our three years at war, Italy is no more the 'owner' of these mountains now than our enemies were before we overcame them. It matters not where the line on the map is drawn, we belong to the mountains, not the mountains to us.

I am a man of the Tyrol. I bow to and adore the elemental power of the Dolomites. And yet, despite the decisive battle of Vittorio Veneto, I am no longer at peace in the mountains. I was a young man when our war began. Three years later, I was broken. The things I saw men do amid those peaks and valleys, the horrors that befell my countrymen; *Mio Dio*, it almost wiped beauty from the landscape and my mind forever. And yet, for Julietta, I passed through those same mountains each spring, in spite of the memories they held.

My plough horse, Alessandro, always recognised the approach of Easter. Of the two of us, he was the one restless to take to the road north. He had no fear of mountains and stamped and tossed his mane with impatience as I loaded him with provisions.

Alessandro knew his way; I barely had to employ the reins. He took us from sea level into the clouds and for ten days we travelled, almost alone on the twisting mountain roads and paths, stopping at inns each evening. He may not have been elegant but Alessandro was a steady horse and he moved with optimism and a love for the trail that I had lost.

Everything heals.

Every abrasion. Every bruise. Every incision.

By dusk my body is whole once more. Neither the memory of what they do to me in the darkest watches of the night, however, nor the pain of each new procedure, is reduced in any degree. And, to my shame, the sickness that brought me here persists through it all – why wouldn't it? They feed it the way a shivering traveller feeds a fire.

Each time they leave me, bleeding, hoarse and exhausted, I tell myself I shall not fear them. *Caro Dio in cielo*, how I try to make myself strong against them, how I delude myself that I will not scream the following night. But when I hear their footfalls in the tunnels, telegraphing their eagerness to be about their work, I run with sweat.

Perhaps this is hell. Was I killed in battle only to begin a sentence of cyclical agonies? I consider that often but such questions will lead me swiftly into madness. If there is a way out, I must concentrate my mind upon it, not abandon myself to fear.

Ten days.

The rush of meltwater, whether a trickle or a cascade, was the sound behind all others. Alessandro clopped through clear bright air, through fog and rain, even a late snow flurry or two. I kept my eyes to the road ahead, praying and thinking of happier times to ward off the ghosts of war. Sometimes I heard the echoed report of artillery or the crack of a rifle on the wind and, even now, I am not sure whether it was real or not.

The only thing that made the journey bearable were the many shrines to *La Madonna*, placed along the steeper paths so that travellers might take strength from her. This I did at every opportunity, always leaving offerings of the smooth, dark pebbles that form the shore of my lakeside home. Alessandro was patient with me at these times, waiting and watching quietly. How I loved him then; my dependable companion without whom the journey could not have been attempted.

At night I perspired and twisted my bedclothes into ropes. I awoke, choking or on the verge of a scream, many times. I would lie there wishing I was back on the gentle shores of Lake Garda, watching the endless shimmering ripples and letting the water wash away my bloody deeds and memories forever.

We made excellent time. Two more days would see us trotting along the avenue of spruce trees lining the steep track to the farm Julietta had laboured so hard to convert: l'orfanotrofio de San Nicola. Her smiling, careworn face. Her wonderful cooking. The many children with bright eyes and shy smiles. I couldn't wait.

But near the Austrian border, I almost turned back.

We were climbing an older trail; narrow, steep and too high up to be regularly maintained. Yet Alessandro's hooves were sure and steady, even in the places where rushing meltwater had cut deep runnels into the track. Our side of the mountain had been in shadow for much of the day and a merciless wind now cut into us. I stopped to cover Alessandro's nose with a protective muzzle and unrolled my cavalry cloak. I pulled it over my travelling clothes, fastening the lower portion to my legs to save my knees from icing up.

The wind was alive and cruel. It resisted us like a tide but Alessandro never once faltered. After an hour we reached a group of stunted, weather-bent pines. No trees could grow above this altitude and I remembered the shelter of these ancient evergreens fondly; built into the mountainside nearby was one of the finest shrines along our path. Though the roads were left to crumble, the face of *La Madonna* was always freshly painted, ever glowing and kind. Alessandro knew the place too – if nothing else it would give us respite from the wind – and he broke into a trot to take us there.

I knew something was wrong before we reached the shrine. Its paint, usually the only bright colour in the still-slumbering landscape, was muted and dull; the statue itself barely visible among the rocks. As we neared it, the wind dropped, wheezing through the pines like the breath of a madman. Alessandro stamped and tried to turn but I held his reins, staring. I felt the sudden quiver in his muscles and, before he could rear, I leapt down and hauled him away. Securing him to a sturdy trunk, I offered him a carrot from his pack. He refused, snorting and wild-eyed.

I stroked his trembling neck and turned back towards the shrine.

"Wait here, old friend."

I was nauseous even before I understood. I knew these colours well. The paint had not faded, nor had *La Madonna* been neglected. Someone had bathed the virgin in blood. It was not some scant, haphazard drizzle. They had collected their offering, very fresh it must have been, and with a jug or bucket had baptised our lady.

War has shown me plenty of spilled gore, *vecchio*, but the sight of that desecration brought me out in sickened hives. The blood was human and I knew what must have been done in order to harvest it. The shrine remained tacky in places where it had pooled. Perhaps only an hour had passed since whoever made this 'offering' had departed.

I glanced back at Alessandro, usually so placid, and his wide eyes begged me to mount up so that we could be on our way. He stamped hard and heaved at his tethered reins. It was my Catholic duty to cleanse the shrine but I knew the smell and the waiting would drive Alessandro crazy before I finished.

I crossed myself and whispered a prayer before hurrying back to him. I wanted nothing other than to go home but I was suddenly more frightened for poor, solitary Julietta than I had ever been before. Whoever had done this was at large. If ever my sister needed someone to shield her, now was the time. We were within two days' ride of the orphanage – less if I pushed Alessandro. With a creak of frost-hardened leather, I hauled myself into the saddle.

"We must persevere, my friend. The next valley will see us into Austria."

To my surprise, Alessandro, broke into a trot the moment I gave him his head. With a courage worthy of the finest horse, he hurried up the trail, past the bloodied virgin and towards our destination.

The doctor pours warm water into a cracked basin, removes his cufflinks and rolls up his sleeves.

His fingers are slim and delicate, the nails manicured, his skin pale. The tiny flaxen hairs on the backs of his hands create a rich lather and he soaps all the way to his elbows. When he rinses, there is neither dirt nor scum, nor do his hands bear a single scar or callus. He dries them thoroughly on a clean white towel and turns towards me.

A surgical mask covers much of his face but I can see the bushy, snow-blond beard and ice-blue eyes; eyes which dart, focus and concentrate on many things but never meet mine. Even his lashes are almost white. I saw so many like him in my three years at war in the mountains – ended so many of their lives, both from a distance and at close quarters. I test the restraints and they give a little but not enough. The leather complains like a warped floorboard and the doctor starts away from me. He barks an order at his two masked assistants; hulking men, neither delicate nor clean.

"Examine the straps, gentlemen."

"We checked 'em already."

"Do it again, please. And tighten the floor bolts."

The assistants shrug and busy themselves around me. From a distance they smell of sweat and illegal liquor. Close up, there's more. One of them is sick and doesn't yet know it. The disease will consume his flesh and kill him within a year. My restraints prevent me from turning my head away. All I can do is breathe through my mouth but that is equally abhorrent – I can taste them too. Their sebum, their pheromones, what they are digesting, every exudation of tainted moisture and unclean breath.

When they're finished, all the slack in the leather bindings is taken up and the chair is anchored to the floor. Under other circumstances I could break through these bonds but Dr. Gustav Weber is no fool. He feeds me enough to ensure productivity, not enough to make me strong.

He steps into view now, not to engage but to assess, as he does each night. He chatters to himself, writing notes in a journal decorated with papier mache roses – his wife's work? A daughter, perhaps? He touches my temple with those artistic, exploratory fingers. Unable to pull away, I close my eyes.

"Lesions have all healed." His accent sickens me. I clench my teeth. "No trace of yesterday's extensive haematoma. Swelling has resolved. Facial tissue appears entirely unblemished."

His sham science mutterings are the same every night; elevating the tension before the real work begins, ensuring he gets what he wants. He pinches the flesh of my cheek.

"The subject is a little pallid today, a little drawn. In order to facilitate a reasonable yield, we will introduce..." He flicks back through the pinkly decorated notebook. "Let us say... two quarts."

I stop shaking immediately. My breathing, high and rapid with fear, settles into a deep, powerful rhythm. What little strength I have concentrates itself in my muscles. The doctor addresses his two accomplices with some impatience.

"I said two quarts, gentlemen. We really *don't* have all night."

His hulking lackeys glance at each other.

"Two quarts'll tap this one out."

Weber barely looks up from his notes.

"So be it. I'll require another by this time tomorrow."

"You got it, Doc."

They lumber through a rough opening into an adjoining chamber, similarly hewn out of solid rock. From where I sit, there's little more I can tell about the room but it hardly matters; I know what's in there. I know what they're going to do. Nevertheless, they slide a makeshift door across the entry.

The doctor busies himself at his improvised autoclave; a large cook pot from which protrude the handles and shafts of his instruments. The steam fogs his spectacles and he turns away to wipe them on a white handkerchief. I test the restraints again. They neither give nor creak.

A frantic thumping comes from beyond the wooden barricade.

"Jesus, Clayt! Hold him steady."

"I'm tryin', godammit."

I can smell their captive. He's been down here almost a week. What they've done has weakened him, but a man's final struggles often engender an almost supernatural ferocity. He has nothing left to lose. I can almost see him, tearing his own skin in an effort to free his hands, shaking his head from side to side to topple whatever they've tied him to.

His scream is raw fury and terror. It dislodges his gag. His voice is his only weapon.

"Get away from me, you soulless *fucks*. Think about what you're doing. Think of your families. Think of God. If you kill me it can never be undone."

To my surprise, there is silence now. As though they are considering his words. The doctor slams down his notebook and marches to the opening.

"Open the door!"

"We can handle it, Doc." Whoever says this doesn't sound convinced. "Won't take but a minute."

Doctor Weber's voice drops to a hiss.

"Open it."

The heavy wooden panel scrapes the ground as they pull it clear. The doctor storms through and out of sight.

"Give me that, you imbecile."

The captive thrashes against his bindings once again. Louder. Harder.

"No," he whispers, incredulity overtaking his terror for a moment. "Not you. Please Dr. Weber, you don't have to do this. Don't you remember me? You delivered our daughter, for Christ's sake."

The doctor doesn't reply.

"Doctor, I'm begging you. Please don't. Who's... going to care for my family? No. *Please*." The voice breaks into a scream again.

"Struggle all you want. Scream all you want." The doctor's voice is gentle, placatory. As though he's telling the man that this medication will make him all better. "It won't make any difference down here."

I hear a pattering. I smell... that smell. I remember the desecrated shrine and I have to stifle a giggle at the absurdity of all this. How good, honest men can be turned from a righteous path, how clear waters can become so muddied.

The pattering slows to a dripping and stops.

The three of them return, liberally stained by their work; the two larger men's faces almost as pale as their masks. My body is rigid as the doctor approaches. I turn away from the smell. From the colour.

"Oh, don't pretend you don't want it" says the doctor. "Surely, after all this time we are beyond charades. You can't sit there and tell me in all honesty that you're not... hungry."

I swear, if I survive this, if it takes me a decade

to find a way out, I will slaughter these men and their families and everyone who has crossed me in this hellish land. Greed has no boundary here and God no dominion. There are those who take and those who suffer to endure them. And that principle is everything this nation and this town is built upon. I cannot let it be so.

I will not allow these deeds to go unanswered.

"I curse you, Weber."

The corners of his eyes wrinkle; a smile behind the surgical mask.

"Open up, *meine kleine soldat*. Open up like a good boy and take your medicine." His assistants clasp my face and force a wooden spatula between my teeth, prising my jaws apart. The doctor forces a length of greased rubber tubing into my mouth causing me to gag. I resist it with my tongue, do my best to clamp my throat closed. But they win. They always do.

I feel the tube enter my stomach. The doctor begins to pour his prescribed two quarts into a funnel held high above my head. My stomach expands.

"Gentlemen, the lights, if you please."

My world turns white.

I am not myself now.

Or perhaps I am more myself than ever I was before. Certainly, the good doctor and his oafish assistants regard me with some mix of fear and revulsion as they perform their operations. The brightness hurts my eyes but I can't stop myself from watching what they do through cracked lids.

I am surrounded by a latticework of crystalline light that emits a haze of blue. The air around me fizzes with electrical potential. Doctor Weber and his men pass through the bars of light without harm each time they approach me and that, more than the fist or the scalpel or the needle, is what causes me to cringe.

First, the doctor sends in the muscle. They take it in turns, like they're digging a trench on a hot day; each one labouring until he's sweating and panting. They wear brass to save their knuckles.

Can you imagine, *vecchio*, what it is like to have your face broken so totally that you become aware of the haemorrhaging inside your own brain? And what it is like for such injuries *not* to be fatal; nor for the blood that inevitably clogs your airways *not* to suffocate you? Can you understand, even for a moment, the rage that germinates and flourishes as you spit out your shattered teeth and survive a beating that would end the life of any other living thing?

Whether you can or not, that is what the good doctor wanted from me: impotent wrath and the resulting alterations in my blood chemistry. When his henchmen are slumped in the corner, sharing a bottle of moonshine, too tired even to speak, only then does Doctor Gustav Weber step through the bars of my light-cage and pierce me with his instruments; when my heart is beating so fast I can't count the beats, when my breathing is so rapid and shallow it sounds like the sniffing of a hound, when all the pain it is possible to feel and all the frenzy and insanity the human vessel can contain has risen within me, that is when he bleeds me. Bleeds me until I am almost as white as the lights he uses to ensure his own safety. But my blood is not enough for the good doctor. Through a hole in the back of the chair, he inserts thick hypodermics between my lower vertebrae to drain off my cerebrospinal fluid.

Freezing and barely conscious, aware of the still-leaking incisions to the arteries in my wrist and neck, I watch him through an agonised smear of vision. He works with what he's taken, spinning my body's red water in vials until it separates, adding unknown liquids, treating the result with heat and light and sealing the final clear fluid in tiny blue bottles.

I ask you, *vecchio*, can you understand my rage now? Can you understand what it has led me to do?

The old man regarded the stranger through the smoke that rose from the fire.

"What does it matter whether I understand or not? If it's absolution you seek, you have travelled in vain."

The stranger's eyes were wide and white with his memories. His entire body quivered with fury. The old man retracted one hand into the folds of his skins and blankets, there to find the handle of his knife.

The stranger, his voice barely a whisper yet dripping threat, said:

"Why do you dismiss me so? How can you shrug off what I have told you? I came in *peace* to this land. I have found nothing here but cruelty and avarice beyond my comprehension."

The old man relaxed. He let go of the knife and his hand reappeared. He tapped out the pipe bowl and refilled it.

"You are just one man, stranger," he said as he lit the fragrant, tarry mix of herbs. "And what has been done to you is as nothing beside what the white invader has done to my people."

"You can't hold me responsible for that."

"No? You endanger my kind by your very presence. I do not care about the injustice and violence you have undergone because you do not care about mine. Like every other white man before you, you have come here only for what you can take. You are just one more wayward cretin, representative of a race more doomed even than my own. How you are able to survive in a world you do not understand has always been a source of astonishment to me. You have spilled into this land like a tide of parasites, devouring everything you happen upon. And here you sit, stranger, asking me if I understand what it is to be abused and beaten and robbed of everything I hold dear. Do not question me again."

The desert lived on in silence.

The stranger leant forward.

"I am sorry. I truly am. I did not think that…" his rage departed, the stranger's eyes were pleading. "Forgive me, *vecchio*. Forgive my anger. But I have died a hundred times to sit before you and beg for a cure."

"You have not died yet, stranger. You have merely suffered." The old man proffered the pipe. "Smoke more. Take it in deep. And finish your story."

Alessandro's pace was such that we reached the orphanage towards the end of the following afternoon. The valley where Virgen lies is steep-sided. The sun arrives late and departs early, leaving the town in a prolonged twilight at the head and tail of each day. Why Julietta felt this was the place for her to perform the Lord's charitable work, I never felt able to ask. Whatever the reason, she was the only light in that oppressive Austrian gloom.

We arrived when the avenue of spruces leading to her large, draughty retreat was already deep in shadow. Alessandro stopped at the entry to the tree-lined track. I leaned forward in the saddle and stroked the side of his powerful neck.

"Come on, old friend. Almost there now. I'm sure Julietta will have a sack of oats for you."

At the mention of oats, Alessandro walked on but his pace was hesitant.

"So much for your stout heart…"

I said it in jest but the words came out weak and tiny in the chill of the afternoon, as though I had not spoken at all. I urged Alessandro forward. Through the trees to my right, I saw a flicker of movement and heard the snap of a twig. Alessandro started away from the noise, snorting. I focused into the gloom.

Whatever moved beyond the spruces was now still. It peered at us, three quarters obscured by a knobbled trunk. Its eyes concentrated the weak afternoon light, iridescing as they locked with mine. Such a thin, slight frame. So many Austrian men had been slaughtered in the war, I thought perhaps it might be a young woman hunting small game. That first impression could not have been more misguided. The figure watched us. It was neither furtive nor shy. Its eyes were those of a stalker. I spurred Alessandro then; something I'd never done in all the years I'd owned him.

"Go. For both our sakes, old friend. Go as fast as you can."

It was my words more than the nip of steel that he responded to. Alessandro broke into the first and only gallop I ever saw him perform. He pounded up the rough track like thunder and I loved him then more than ever.

When the austere architecture of the orphanage came into view, with its sombre stone walls and black-eyed windows, I had never felt such relief. Not even after battle.

I secured Alessandro loosely to a fence post and rapped on the door. All was quiet. I waited a few moments. Glancing back down the darkening avenue, I was filled with an uncommon and irrational dread. To hell with it, I thought, whether they are eating or sleeping, I needed to be on the other side of the sturdy door.

When there came no answer to my increasingly panicked hammering, I stepped back from the door and looked up at the windows. Thinking I saw a small, pale face I called up.

"Could you tell the mistress of the house that—"

But the figure stepped out of view, leaving me to question whether I'd seen anything other than the refection of a cloud in the glass. The afternoon grew dimmer. I drew my cavalry cloak tight around me and untethered Alessandro.

"At least we can get you settled in for the evening."

I led him to the rear of the orphanage. The farm had been a hospital during the war but Julietta, a nurse there, had seen another use for it once the Austrian wounded had returned to their families. Why she could not have done this work in Veneto remained a mystery to me but such behaviour typified Julietta. She was a strong, beautiful woman who could have had her pick of our returning soldiers – or even the wealthier sons of Italy who had found ways to avoid the fighting. Instead, she lived across the border with only her faith for a bedfellow and the forty or so children for whom the orphanage was a temporary home.

I found oats in the stable and gave a generous helping to Alessandro in a nosebag. Of Julietta's three horses there was no sign. If she'd been forced to sell them, things must have become desperate during the intervening year.

Whatever the case, Alessandro had the rich, floury grains to himself.

The sound of his contented chewing diminished as I walked into the courtyard behind the orphanage. The place was deserted. I would at least have expected the raucous sound of children playing games. There was nothing. I wondered if they had been visited by Spanish influenza. Many of my comrades in arms, not killed by lead or shrapnel or frost, had died of flu and I knew the same disease had ravaged Austria. I crossed myself, whispering a prayer to *La Madonna* as I traversed the courtyard.

I halted before I reached the door to the kitchens.

There was a stain on the cobbles, as though they were dark with rain. But I knew this stain well from the battlefield. Enough blood had been spilled here to signify a death. I placed my cold fingertips to my mouth. My only option, it seemed then, would be to ride Alessandro back down the track and seek both news and assistance in Virgen.

I took a deep breath and turned back to the stables but my way was barred. Julietta stood there, so close our faces almost touched. I had been so consumed with worry, I didn't even hear her approach.

"Paolo," she said and threw her arms around my neck. I flinched at the fierceness of her kisses. When she stood back, she was smiling and radiant, her skin pale and flawless, the only shining thing in that dismal valley.

Her face soon creased with concern when she looked into my eyes.

"What is it, Paolo? What is wrong?"

With one hand, I gestured towards the damp shadow on the cobblestones.

"I...I thought..."

Laughing, she took my arm and led me towards the kitchen.

"Do not fear, brother. Take a grappa with me. I have much to tell you."

The stranger blinked as he exhaled and handed the pipe over the dying coals to the old man.

"Everything I recount... It's as though I'm there again. Right there in that time and moment."

The old man nodded.

"That is good."

"But I don't want to go back. Not to any of it."

The stranger looked around, into the impenetrable desert darkness. "There is blood here, too." He said. "Blood everywhere I go. I cannot escape it."

The old man smoked and returned the pipe across the fire.

"None of us can. This world spins on blood. Every action demands a sacrifice, the releasing of a little life."

The stranger stared at their surroundings as though lost.

"What are we smoking, old man?"

"Sacred plants. Those that free and purify us. Those that... stimulate."

"Why? Why can we not simply speak and be done with it?"

"Because your intentions must be sent into spirit. Only in smoke, in *form*, can your words reach beyond the world we see. That is how purification is achieved."

The stranger shook his head, half snorting, half giggling. He drew hard on the pipe.

One night they came to the chamber trailing fumes of liquor. As he prepared for business the doctor knocked his entire tray of instruments to the floor.

He stood there, swaying.

"Butterfingers," he said eventually and his hulking assistants broke into giggles, collapsing against each other to keep from falling over. The doctor gathered everything up and dumped it back into the tray. A scalpel blade must have touched him; I spotted the cut before he even knew he'd done it. Only when he saw where my gaze was levelled did he look down.

"*Scheiße*"

How my heart quickened, how my muscles swelled and my sinews tightened, to see the man bleed.

His eyes became slits. He pulled down his surgical mask and the assistants stopped giggling.

"Uh, boss... you said we shouldn't—"

"Silence, *dummkopf*. Turn on the lights and examine the bindings."

One oaf fumbled the switches while the other peered at my straps. The cage of humming, blue light sprang into form around me. In it, Dr. Gustav Weber's face was pale and ugly, his eyes full of hate. He leaned in and I saw the abhorrent purity of his white-blond lashes and frosty beard, his moist lips inviting destruction. I would have prayed for the strength to free myself and tear him apart but God was long dead to me by then, and I to Him.

"It seems appropriate that a dirty, snivelling Italian carries the sickness you are cursed with. And equally fitting that a noble, pure-blooded Austrian should be the one to transform your affliction into a life-giving elixir."

He straightened and turned to the tray of unclean implements. The bars of light crackled as he passed through them. When he returned, he held not a scalpel or needle but a small, sickle-shaped blade in his still-bleeding right hand. He gestured to the chamber's roof with his eyes.

"It's a different world up there now, dago. People with previously incurable ailments are being healed by the filth in your veins. I extract your blood and split the regenerative elements from the disease itself. Heat treatment and containment in a solution of grape alcohol annihilates the virulence, leaving a tincture so potent it will cure any illness you can name. It even re-grows limbs in amputees and heals bullet wounds. Can you imagine what this will lead to? *Weber's Solution* is already selling like no other medicine ever formulated."

The doctor held up the knife, catching a beam of light and reflecting it into my face. I screamed, instantly blinded. I smelled my seared eyelids, smoke rising from that brief caress of light.

"Butterfingers," said the doctor. "You know, all this demand is putting quite a strain on our little cottage industry. Fortunately, the ratio of curative fluid to alcohol in my preparation is minuscule. Ironic, isn't it, that your diseased plasma can be such a power for good? But, as I was saying, the factory is working at high output and the workers need to rest." He paused, directing his voice across the chamber. "Isn't that correct, gentlemen?"

"Uh... sure, boss."

There was a pause.

"We need a little recreation," whispered the doctor.

I heard him step back. I heard the rattle of steel on his tray.

"Take your pick, gentlemen. Whatever piques your curiosity. Please, be my guest."

After some hesitation, I heard them stagger to the workbench, heard the clatter of work-hardened fingers fumbling for purchase on instruments designed for smaller, more dextrous hands.

"Remove a man's sight and his remaining senses become so much more acute, isn't that right, my grubby little Italian friend?" I heard the doctor approach. "Go on, Gentlemen. Don't be shy. Step right up and have your fun. I think we've all earned the night off. Even our obliging friend here."

They started with my fingers.

It was after they'd gone, having exhausted themselves with cruelty, that I realised there was a way out.

Blinded, and every part of me a choir of suffering, I became aware of something about my body for the first time. The pieces that had been severed and trodden into the ground were still alive. They, too, had awareness – I could sense their pain just as I felt it in the stumps and sockets where they had so recently been. My blood was the key; it was strong. It could survive being separated from me. Wherever my blood was, that was my body *and* my consciousness.

I floated on an ocean of agony. Having been attended to, not only with brass knuckles, surgical instruments and work boots, but with bottle shards and the headless handle of a sledgehammer, I was a pulped carcass; inanimate, my brain swollen inside my shattered skull.

Yet I had an awareness beyond all of that, something larger and more diffuse that was above my ruined, separated body and at the same time within each part of it. I tried shifting my perspective and found I was able to leave what remained of my torso and enter my left thumb, which had been kicked under my chair. I slipped from there into my pummelled and partially shredded liver. From my liver to a broken tooth. From the tooth to the ruptured contents of my scrotum.

I cannot boast that torture and dismemberment suited me, but I realised then that it was no impediment. As my daily regeneration began, the scorching of my eyes receded and I found myself mesmerised by a warm orange glow. I was staring at the tiny window of the incinerator in which something yet burned. As my body renewed itself, my broad net of awareness diminished. My severed parts were dying, all consciousness returning to my core.

Before the process of centralisation was complete, I forced my awareness to expand. Two fingers, boot-flattened and dirty, lay directly in front of my chair. I reached out to them. A neatly excised section of ribcage – the good doctor's handiwork – rested near the leg of the work table. A bloody pair of pliers had been discarded next to my grit-crusted tongue. I united them all, bending them to a common purpose before the blood within them died.

When Gustav Weber returned with his men, he appeared embarrassed. Not so much by what they'd done to me, but by the fact that they had left such a mess. With orders almost whispered, the doctor busied himself cleaning and sterilising his instruments while the oafs stoked the incinerator to a blaze and swept up my remains. They threw every severed part into the fire but, by then, I had what I needed.

I took not one grappa with Julietta but several. By the time she had recounted recent events at the orphanage, my face was hot and the kitchen, where we sat near the wood-fired stoves, wavered whenever I glanced around. The stain in the courtyard was pig's blood, nothing more.

But l'orfanotrofio di San Nicola *had* been visited by sickness.

"If it has been passed from one child to another," I said, "it must be some kind of influenza. Lord knows, the flu has taken enough Italians to give Saint Peter the vapours."

Julietta shook her head.

"Flu is a febrile illness, Paolo. None of the children have shown a trace of fever. If anything, the converse is true. They are cold to the touch."

"Perhaps this flu is... different."

"No. It's something else."

I went back over her story in my mind.

"You said a priest came some weeks ago."

"Yes. He brought the child Larissa whose parents had died in a fire in Lienz."

"Was the priest unwell?"

Julietta smirked.

"He was a portly fellow. He seemed out of breath simply from riding his mule. However, I could see nothing wrong with him."

"What about the girl?"

"Like they always are. Quiet. Pale. Forlorn. I loved her from the moment I saw her."

"But it was after the priest left her with you that the illness began to take hold?"

Julietta thought about it for a moment.

"A week later. Perhaps two."

I sighed.

"One more grappa," I said, slurring. "And then I must rest. God willing I will sleep through until morning and feel reborn."

Julietta placed her cool fingers over mine. The chill opposed the alcoholic heat in my blood and I drew away in shock. I saw the hurt in her expression, quickly denied, disappearing like a pebble into a lake. Lonely Julietta. She smiled at me and I thought of how the children of the orphanage must have felt when smiled upon like that. As though they had found a mother more benevolent and beautiful than their own.

I stood, steadied myself, and made for the door, turning back before I reached it.

"It's been a difficult crossing this time, Julietta. I'm sorry to be so... anxious. It is very good to see you again. I'm glad we've spoken and I know that I shall be less troubled in the morning."

"Paolo."

Her face was hard to read.

"What is it?"

She stood up, swept across the kitchen and embraced me. Her tendons quivered with the intensity of it. When she stepped away she was crying.

"I'm so very glad you came to us." She took my hand and led me into the gloom of the downstairs corridor, suddenly strong and forthright once again. "Come, brother. I have prepared a better room for you this year. Further from the children and with a view of the valley. It is quiet. I know you'll rest well there."

Rest: how, in waking, I dreamed of it; the deepest, blackest sleep imaginable. I stumbled after her.

"*Vecchio*, please, I implore you. Do not make me tell it all."

"There is no other way. The great spirit knows what you've done but if you cannot speak it, here beneath the stars where his desert ears can hear you, then you are not ready."

The stranger's eyes flashed, their whites catching what little light now rose from the almost spent fire. As quickly as the anger flared, it was gone. He hung his head for long, silent moments and the old man watched, intent.

The stranger lifted his head. He took a deep breath.

How I wish it had been nothing but a dream. Indeed, for a while I was able to convince myself that was what it was. Until I, too, became sick.

In the fathomless night, when time is endless and meaningless, I became aware of movement. It might have been someone crossing the corridor. Perhaps the wind forcing itself though the spaces around the windows. So tired was I that it was easy to ignore the disturbance. I fell back into slumber almost immediately.

An age later, I felt a chill invade the warmth of my bed. Even then, such was my exhaustion and grappa-induced stupor, I did not wake fully enough to respond. I felt no pain or discomfort but I began to sense that I was no longer alone – neither in my room, nor in my bed. It was as though wild creatures had crept in at the windows to take refuge under the covers with me. Feral things with Tyrolean frost in their fingertips.

Even when their teeth pierced my skin, I could not rouse myself. The pangs of penetration were brief and almost painless, barely the softest of nips. There was warmth after that; a slick stickiness at my elbows and groin, the slippery insistence of tongues playing over my skin. I thought the war had killed every spark of physical passion within me, blasted it to dust along with my peace of mind, but now the flicker of intimate desire rose like a candle flame and heat burst across my body. I began to move against the lapping, to invite my flesh for bites. I began to thrust.

It was then that I awoke, the room aglow with moonlight, to find my bed squirming with the pale bodies of children, the orphans of whom there had been no sign when I arrived. My first response was animal delight. The weight and touch of their bodies was a circus of sensation. More of them thronged the bedside, clamouring for their turn. In the next moment, I was reviled both by my godless salacity and the reality of what the children were doing to my body.

Their tiny teeth had sunk deeply but painlessly into many superficial blood vessels and now, like kittens at the saucer, they lapped at the red wellings. It had not been a neat performance; the sheets were darkly streaked.

"Get away from me!"

That was what I intended to scream with every cell in my body but all that escaped me was a half-formed breath. Insane with panic, I tried to buck the children from my body. There was a slight twitch and jerk in my muscles but if the orphans noticed the movement they gave no sign. The cold from their bodies began to penetrate mine. No longer was the sensation pleasant or titillating. They were draining me.

And then that voice, the sweet angelic voice of my saviour, Julietta.

"Children!" she screeched, and every orphan in the room became statuesque. "What is the meaning of this abomination? How *dare* you touch my brother?" Her tone was venomous. Even I was afraid of the power in it. "Return to your rooms immediately and await your punishment – it will be a monument to suffering, you vile, motherless vermin."

I might have laughed at the way the children left my room, leaping over each other's naked backs like rats and scurrying away into the dark corridors of the orphanage. Julietta, her face softening in the moonlight, approached me. Her face creased as she assessed the many puncture wounds on my body and the amount of life I had leaked into the bed.

She shook her head and knelt beside me.

"I'm so sorry, Paolo. This is an outrage."

I tried to answer but I had no strength.

"I should have told you not to come this year but I did so hope your arrival would change things... that you could help me."

Her cool fingers caressed the bites as though her touch might heal them.

"You're so cold, Paolo."

She slipped into bed beside me and pulled the covers over us. A little warmth returned. I tried to thank her but I could neither move nor make a sound. I stared up into the darkness. Julietta fluttered her delicate fingertips over my weeping wounds.

"Oh, *mio* Paolo. *Mio bel fratello*. I have become so alone here in the mountains."

She retreated beneath the covers, her frigid lips leaving icy delight wherever they met my skin, until she reached what was forbidden. Her mouth was cool and wet and muscular. I imagined it as the inside of a serpent. The serpent bit me, the final bite, and there she fed. Willingly, I gave all I had; all I could.

A dream, *vecchio*. That was what I told myself. And, for a while, I could believe it. For in the dream I believed myself dead and that I would never wake again. But wake I did. Before dawn, I saddled Alessandro and we fled back to the border

It was then that I discovered how the sunlight scalds. The deep, gloomy valleys of the Dolomites suited me well after that. From afternoon until late the following morning I was able to travel in daylight's shadow.

My strength and speed soon became far greater than Alessandro's. From then on I led him by his reins. I wish I could say that I fed only upon the animals I caught each night; the marmots and foxes and bats. But I found myself as void of morality as my sister and her tribe of parasitic strays. I bled the cattle and sheep I found, bled them dry. Women and children too, whenever I could gain easy access to them. High in the Tyrolean passes, though, where no such sustenance was available, I made use of Alessandro for as long as I could.

What a noble horse and friend he was.

Returning to Pieve and the soothing waters of Lake Garda brought me no peace. I was sick; depraved. Each evening, the moment the sun dipped below the horizon, I sought out priests in the churches of Veneto, looking for a cure.

There is no true charity in the Christian faith, *vecchio*. A fact I'm sure you're well-acquainted with. The instant a padre heard my confession, he would either sound the alarm or try to end me himself. It is of enormous regret to me that I was forced to silence so many holy men. On the other hand, many of them deserved to have their throats torn out so that I could drink their filthy Catholic blood. We both know, do we not, *vecchio*, what a charade religion is?

There *were* charitable souls in Italy, though. Quiet men. Learned men who understood my sickness and had an idea of how it might be remedied. By and by the trail led me here to America, to New Mexico, to Pandemonium and, after almost six months underground with the doctor and his men, to you.

That, though it shames me, is my story.

Again, they leave me drained and too weak to move.

But the doctor's night of revelry was the only mistake I needed him to make. A scalpel, delivered to me by a grotesque reunion of my own severed remains, now rests between my wrist and the arm of the chair to which it is secured.

Far above me, the darkness loses its battle with the sun, fleeing around the globe to hold dominion elsewhere. The dance is endless. But inside this church of solid stone, this vault of degradation, it is always dark and I, at these eternal vespers, am always safe. My strength returns as my blood rebuilds itself within me. The moment I can move, I wriggle my wrist and move my forearm backwards and forwards inside the straps, working the scalpel into view and within reach of my fingers.

Oh, my dear lost lord above, how good it feels to hold steel in my hand, to be equal to the good doctor at last. I turn the scalpel around and work it against the leather. The hide is tough but it cannot withstand a razor-sharp blade.

There is no hurry. Snick. Rip. Snick. Rip. It will come.

And then, for the first time in many moons, my right hand is free. Releasing my left hand takes moments. The straps at my head, neck, chest, legs and feet are next. I stand, naked but for a blade, and stretch out. I impel the blood to every frozen joint and shortened sinew. My body sings not with agony tonight, but with power.

I check the walls and the door. There is no

way I can break through the steel entrance, bolted as it is from the outside. I enter the second chamber where a woman is chained to a bare brass bed frame. They've cut her two nights running but yet she lives. When she sees me her eyes widen with relief and tears cascade from her cheeks as she tries to speak through her gag. I feed until she is white and cold. The second chamber is little more than a cavern cut from the solid rock. There is no way out.

The doctor and his assistants each carry hand-lights powered by dry cells which shine the same deadly beams that have imprisoned me while they work. Only one of them would need to cast his light upon me and I would be helpless. Even with surprise on my side, there is no way I could fight the three of them and be assured of escape. I've been here too long now to risk recapture. I might never have another chance.

And now I notice that the good doctor, perhaps a little distracted by his recollections of the previous evening, has forgotten his fine silk waistcoat. I stare at it for a long time before moving to the incinerator. The fire, which they riddle and feed and stoke every night, has died down. I open the hatch, noticing with some surprise that its improvised handle, fashioned from a horseshoe, works both on the inside and the outside of the door. I scrape the grate and charred bones fall through. I open the ash compartment below and clean it thoroughly before adding wood and stoking the fire to a roaring blaze.

As the temperature gauge rises, I write a note and leave it on the chair where I have spent close to half a year.

I came in peace to this land, doctor. How shall I depart?

From the instrument tray I take the pliers, fix them over my right upper canine and pull downwards. It takes more strength and determination than I expected but finally, after twisting and levering for several minutes, the tooth comes free with a damp tearing sound. By the light of the tiny window in the incinerator, I examine it; the threads of gum tissue, dull and jellylike, the tooth itself perfect and deadly. My plasma will live on inside it. The tooth will heal. I will heal; in totality.

I place it in the doctor's pocket and drape the

waistcoat over the back of the chair, a chair stained to ebony with my own blood.

By now the temperature inside the incinerator is extreme, hot enough to reduce one more body to ashes. I lift the handle, scalding my palm. The smell of burnt flesh rises.

"Fino a domani, signori."

I take hold of the hatchway and swing into the flames feet first. My skin ignites immediately and smoke rises fast, filling the coffin-shaped space. My hand is on fire as I reach out, swing the door closed behind me and force the handle down. There's no point trying not to scream. As I burn, fully conscious, I become aware of a cool place. A small space. A haven. I send my awareness out and find myself encased in a tiny living refuge of flawless white ivory; a canine. The predator's trademark. The chamber of hewn rock where they have milked my lifeblood each night is cold. It is paradise. The demented screams from within the incinerator go on and on.

I wait.

"That is all there is," says the stranger. "The truth. Everything."

The pipe has long since been set aside. The old man appears drowsy, his eyes downcast, lids three-quarters closed. The stranger leans forward, swaying with the effects of the aromatic fumes.

"*Vecchio*, I beg you. I have shared the pipe with you. I have given my confession. Release me from this curse."

The old man does not move or respond. The fire is almost out and the stars are fading. In the east there is a paleness to the night sky. The stranger tilts his head, leans a little closer. The old man does not appear to be breathing.

It is as the stranger moves to the side of the fire pit, crawling on his hands and knees to take a closer look, that the old man, like the spilled-ink shadow of a cat, lunges forward. His flecked blade is almost invisible as it parts the night air and divides the stranger's ribs.

Equally agile, the stranger leaps away and lands upright.

He laughs.

"This was a pretence, *vecchio*? All you meant to do was kill me? I can't believe I travelled so far to beg help from an idiot."

The old man glances at his hunting knife. The

point drips dark fluid into the dirt. He wipes the blade on his trouser leg and replaces it in its sheath.

"You came to me for healing," says the old man.

The stranger puts a hand to his wound, frowning.

"You can't kill me, old man. I have tasted the fires of hell and I am equal to them. If you cannot help me, I will find someone who can."

The stranger edges towards the old man, his eyes predatory. The old man stands his ground.

"You have taken enough lives, stranger. Only one more death awaits you."

The stranger raises his hands, turns them in front of his face.

"What have you done to me?"

"I have done as you asked."

The stranger collapses to his knees.

"*Santa Maria*, mother of God...help me."

The old man places a hand on the fallen man's shoulder.

"You have acted well. Your story has been heard and you are released."

By the time the stranger hits the ground, he is nothing but a dust-filled suit. The old man places the clothes and shoes on the fire, rekindling brief white flames from the almost spent embers. All that remains is a fine chain from which hangs a silver crucifix of the suffering Christ. The old man weighs it in his palm for a few moments, before casting it into the night.

Also by Joseph D'Lacey:

Novels

Meat (Bloody Books, 2008)
Garbage Man (Bloody Books, 2009)
Blood Fugue (Salt Publishing, 2012)
Black Feathers (Angry Robot, 2013)
The Book of the Crowman (Angry Robot, 2014)
The Veil: Testaments I and II (Horrific Tales
Publishing, 2016)
Clown Wars: Blood & Aspic (with Jeremy Drysdale)
(2016)

Novellas & Novelettes

The Kill Crew (Stonegarden, 2009)
Roadkill (This Is Horror, 2013)

Collections

Splinters (Timeline Books, 2012)

Visit Joseph D'Lacey at his website:
josephdlacey.wixsite.com/josephdlacey

Now available and forthcoming from
Black Shuck Shadows:

Shadows 9 – Winter Freits
                    by Andrew David Barker

Shadows 10 – The Dead
                        by Paul Kane

Shadows 11 – The Forest of Dead Children
                    by Andrew Hook

Shadows 12 – At Home in the Shadows
                    by Gary McMahon

blackshuckbooks.co.uk/shadows